Weekly Reader Presents

Goodnight Wembley Fraggle

(Original Title: Why Wembley Fraggle Couldn't Sleep)

By H. B. Gilmour · Pictures by Barbara McClintock

Muppet Press
Holt, Rinehart and Winston
NEW YORK

Published by Holt, Rinehart and Winston,
383 Madison Avenue, New York, New York 10017.

Library of Congress Cataloging in Publication Data
Gilmour, H. B. (Harriet B.), 1939–
Why Wembley Fraggle couldn't sleep.
"Muppet Press."
Summary: When Wembley can't fall asleep, he bothers
all the other inhabitants of Fraggle Rock by keeping
them awake with him.
1. Children's stories, American.   [1. Sleep—Fiction.
2. Puppets—Fiction]   I. McClintock, Barbara, ill.
II. Title.
PZ7.G43807Wh   1985   [E]   84-19286
ISBN: 0-03-004557-6

First Edition
Printed in the United States of America
1 3 5 7 9 10 8 6 4 2

ISBN 0-03-004557-6

This book is a presentation of
Weekly Reader Books

Weekly Reader Books offers book clubs for children
from preschool through junior high school.

For further information write to:
Weekly Reader Books
4343 Equity Drive
Columbus, Ohio 43228

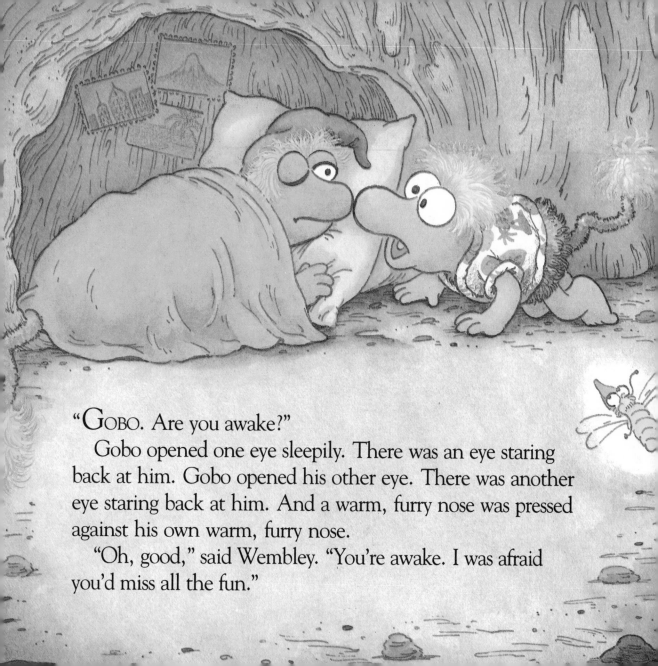

"GOBO. Are you awake?"

Gobo opened one eye sleepily. There was an eye staring back at him. Gobo opened his other eye. There was another eye staring back at him. And a warm, furry nose was pressed against his own warm, furry nose.

"Oh, good," said Wembley. "You're awake. I was afraid you'd miss all the fun."

"What fun?" Gobo yawned and looked around the cozy cave he shared with Wembley. "It's the middle of the night. Go back to sleep, Wembley."

With a sigh, Wembley climbed up the ladder and got into his bed.

Wembley couldn't sleep. For three nights in a row, he'd tossed and turned and worried about what everyone else in Fraggle Rock was doing. *I'll bet they're having a good time,* he thought. *They just never wake me up to tell me.*

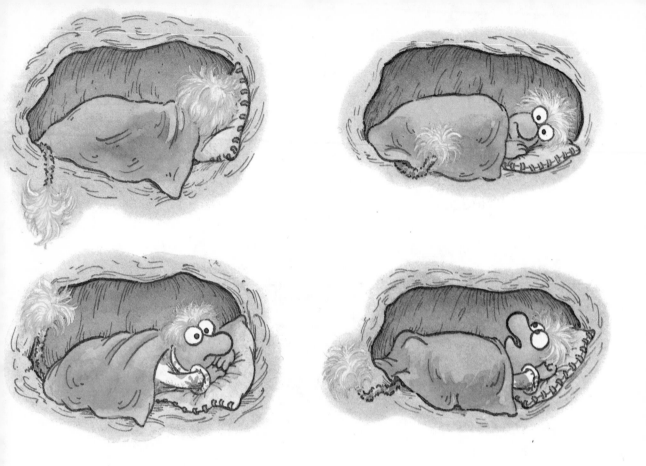

He curled up on his right side. But the bed felt hot. He rolled onto his left side . . . and found a lumpy spot! Lying on his tummy felt crummy. So he stretched out on his back.

"Gobo, how can you sleep?" Wembley whispered from his bed. "Don't you ever worry about all the fun you're missing?"

When there was no answer, Wembley whispered a little louder. "Gobo, do you hear that click-tock, click-tock, click-tock noise?"

"Doozer boots," murmured Gobo. "I told you last night, Wembley—it's just the sound of Doozer boots marching along the rocky ledges."

"Oh, now I remember," said Wembley. He scrambled down the ladder and stood beside Gobo's bed. "Maybe the Doozers are tired," he said. "Do you think they'd like a helping hand?"

Gobo groaned. "I told you the night *before* last, Wembley—Doozers don't get tired. But Fraggles do!"

"Oh," said Wembley with a sigh. Suddenly, he smiled and snapped his fingers. "Then Boober must be tired," he said. "I'll go help him do the laundry right now!"

Gobo sat up. "Wembley," he began. But then he yawned. By the time he'd finished yawning, Wembley was gone.

Gobo rubbed his eyes with his fists. Then he stretched and sighed, and scratched his head. Then he fell over backward, right into his bed.

"Are you going for a trip with your Uncle Traveling Matt?"
Red asked when she and Mokey saw Gobo the next morning.

"No," said Gobo, yawning, "Why do you ask?"

Red giggled. "Because the bags under your eyes look like
they're packed!"

"I wish I *could* pack my bags," Gobo said glumly. "I haven't
gotten a full night's sleep since Wembley started staying awake
all night!"

"Wembley? Then it really *was* him!" Mokey exclaimed.
"The night before last, he woke us to ask if we'd like to go for
a midnight swim."

"I thought I was dreaming," said Red.

"You?" grumbled Boober, joining them at the Fraggle Pond.
"He banged on *my* door last night!"

"Boober, what's wrong with your hat?" Mokey asked.
Boober's old brown cap had taken on an odd new shape.

"My hat is fine, but my head's not." Boober lifted his cap to
reveal a great big lump. "And it's all Wembley's fault!" he said.

"Wembley hit you on the head?" gasped Red.

"No, no," Boober explained. "When Wembley woke me, I hurried to answer the door in the dark, and I slipped on some spilled soufflé."

"Poor Boober," said Mokey.

"Poor all of us," said Red.

"We've got to keep Wembley from staying awake all night," Gobo decided.

"And keeping everyone else awake, too," added Boober.

"Perhaps he's afraid of the dark," Mokey suggested.

Boober disagreed. "Poor nutrition," he said. "Too many moss-burgers before bedtime. Or it could be a lack of vitamin F."

"He doesn't get enough exercise," declared Red. "If he did, he'd be too tired to do anything *but* sleep!"

"It's because he can't make decisions," Gobo decided. "If Wembley just put his mind to it, he could sleep the whole night through!"

"We must try to help him," said Mokey.

"Good idea," agreed Boober. "But let's do it later—after I've had a nap!"

It was nearly nighttime when the Fraggle friends arrived at Wembley's cave. "What a nice surprise," he said. "Now we can have a party. All we need are chips and dips and Doozer sticks."

"Just as I suspected." Boober shook his head. "No wonder you can't sleep, Wembley. Everyone knows that chips and dips and Doozer sticks before bedtime can keep you awake for hours!"

Boober pulled a jar of purpleberry juice from his knapsack. "Two sips of this," he said, "and you'll be fast asleep in no time. Nothing to be afraid of, Wembley. Just watch me."

Boober drank two great gulps of purpleberry juice. Then he yawned, and stretched, and sighed and said, "See!"

Wembley had to agree. Boober *did* look very sleepy.

"I've got an idea that's much more fun," said Red. "You run up and down the ladder to your bed. And you wiggle your nose every time you climb up, and you touch your toes every time you climb down. Here, watch me. I'll show you what I mean."

Up the ladder Red scampered. At the top, she wiggled her
nose. Then down she came and touched her toes. Then up
again. And down. And then . . . Red yawned, and
stretched, and sighed and said, "You see? I'm already sleepy."

"I find nothing as soothing for sleep as a little night music," said Mokey. "So this afternoon at Inspiration Cave, I composed a lullaby especially for you, Wembley. When I sing it, you will relax completely. You will close your weary eyes and rest. And you will think the words and music are fabulous!"

Mokey started to sing her brand-new lullaby. It began: "Go to sleep, Wembley, sweet. Take a load off your feet . . ."

By the time she got to the part that went "All your friends want to do . . . is to get some sleep, too," Mokey's eyes were closed. "You see," she whispered. Then she yawned and stretched. "There's nothing like a lullaby to put a Fraggle to sleep."

Wembley looked around. "Boober and Red and Mokey are nearly fast asleep," he whispered to Gobo. "They're going to miss all the fun."

"What fun?" asked Gobo.

"Why, all the fun that goes on in Fraggle Rock at night," Wembley explained.

"Is that why you've been staying awake all night?" Gobo asked. "Wembley, every Fraggle in Fraggle Rock goes to sleep at night."

"Everyone?" asked Wembley.

"Everyone but you," Gobo sighed.

"I guess I can go to sleep then," Wembley said. "If I still remember how . . ."

"It's easy, Wembley," said Gobo. "All it really takes is a simple decision. You say to yourself, 'Self, it's bedtime. It's boring. There's nothing to do now. I think I'll go to sleep.' Then you close your eyes. Watch me. I'll show you how to do it."

Gobo climbed into his bed and closed his eyes. He said to himself: "Self, it's bedtime. It's boring . . ."
The next thing Wembley knew, Gobo was snoring!

For three nights in a row, Wembley had wondered what he was missing when he slept. He'd been sure all his friends were wide awake and having fun.

Now he knew. He wasn't missing anything. All his best friends went to sleep, too!

Except for Gobo's snoring—and the click-tock of Doozer boots marching along the rocky ledges—the night seemed very still. And the cave seemed very cozy.

Wembley took two sips of Boober's purpleberry juice. Then he climbed up and down his ladder, just as Red had shown him. Then he hummed a few lines of the lullaby Mokey had written especially for him. And finally, surrounded by his sleeping friends, he crawled happily into his bed and closed his eyes.

"Self, it's bedtime," Wembley said. "And it really *is* boring being awake when your best friends are asleep. There's no fun to miss. There's nothing to do. So thanks and good night— to Boober and Red and Mokey and Gobo. And Wembley," he added. "Good night to you, too."